Journey to Japan

Journey to Japan

Stacy Towle Morgan

Illustrated by Pamela Querin

BETHANY HOUSE PUBLISHERS
MINNEAPOLIS, MINNESOTA 55438

Journey to Japan
Copyright © 1997
Stacy Towle Morgan

Cover and story illustrations by Pamela Querin

Published by Bethany House Publishers
A Ministry of Bethany Fellowship, Inc.
11300 Hampshire Avenue South
Minneapolis, Minnesota 55438

Printed in the United States of America.

Library of Congress Cataloging-in-Publication Data

Morgan, Stacy Towle.
    Journey to Japan / by Stacy Towle Morgan.
        p. cm. — (Ruby slippers school ; #5)
    Summary: Hope is not looking forward to visiting Japan, but
when she meets Yoko, a tenth grader who is considered a rebel by
her father, Hope realizes that her worries about earthquakes are not
as important as Yoko's concerns.
    ISBN 1-55661-604-X
    [1. Christian life—Fiction. 2. Japan—Fiction.] I. Title.
II. Series: Morgan, Stacy Towle. Ruby Slippers School ; 5.
PZ7.M82642Jo   1997
[Fic]—dc21
                                                97-4671
                                                 CIP
                                                   AC

To our friend
and sister in Christ, Yoko.

STACY TOWLE MORGAN has been writing ever since she was eight, when she set up a typewriter in the closet of the room she shared with her sister. A graduate of Cedarville College and Western Kentucky University, Stacy has written many feature articles and several books for children. Stacy and her husband, Michael, make their home in Indiana, where she currently spends her days home-schooling their four school-aged children in their own Ruby Slippers School.

Ruby Slippers School

9702

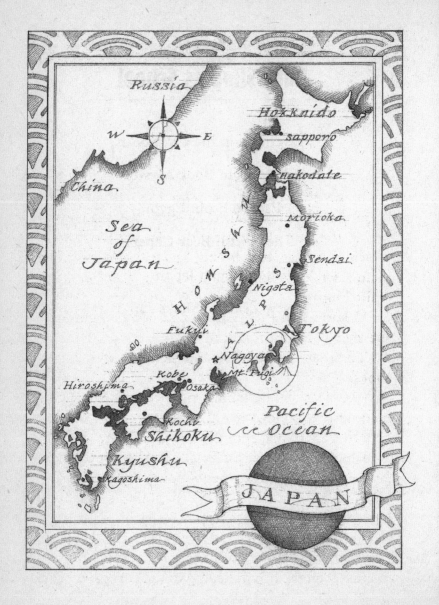

Prologue

It was the first day of school in my neighborhood. Annie and I walked down to the bus stop to see all the new clothes the kids on the block were wearing. Annie's best friend, Susan, had on a green plaid skirt and a light yellow sweater over her crisp, white blouse.

"I know that I'll be steaming hot by lunchtime," she said. "But I just had to wear it today."

Then she smiled big and pointed at her new shoes.

"My feet will be killing me by lunch, too!" She held up two Band-Aids. "I probably won't even be able to walk home from the bus without these."

I looked down at Susan's feet, then at Annie's. Annie was still wearing her slippers.

"Maybe you should just wear slippers to school, like Annie," I suggested.

Annie's face turned red, and she started giggling. "Well, at least they're comfortable."

Just then the bus pulled up to the corner. We saw

Alex and Austin Mullins racing toward us at full speed. "Wait for us!" they yelled.

They bounded up the high black steps. Susan and the other neighbors waved good-bye to us. The bus driver leaned forward to grab the handle to shut the door. "Are you girls going to school or not?"

I took Annie's hand and smiled. "Yes, sir. But our school is just down the street."

"Thanks anyway," Annie added.

We turned and headed back to our house, ready to start a new year at the Ruby Slippers School.

Chapter One

I s that you, girls?" Dad called from his office.

We walked over to the doorway. Dad was sitting at his desk with a cup of coffee in his hands. He was wearing the sweat shirt Annie and I had made for him last Christmas. It had our handprints all over it.

"Hey, you two," he said. "I know this is only the first day of school for you, but how would you like to go to a *different* school?"

"What?!" we both said, surprised.

"Do you mean we can't stay in home-school anymore?" Annie asked.

"No, no, no," Dad said, laughing. "I just wondered if you might like to visit a school—for a day—in another country."

I was relieved.

"Where are we going?" I asked.

"Well, come over here, and I'll show you."

Dad put down his cup of coffee and reeled his chair around to face the globe. I loved his globe. Sometimes at night, I would sneak down to his office and sit in his chair. Then I would close my eyes and put both hands on the globe and start it spinning.

I loved feeling the bumps that showed the mountains and trying to guess where my hands would be when the spinning stopped. "Nigeria," I would say to myself—then find my finger had settled instead on the western coast of South America. It was a great game.

"Right here, in Japan," Dad said.

Japan! That's so far away, I thought. I didn't know much about Japan, and I wasn't sure I wanted to go and find out.

"What's wrong, Hope?" Dad said. "You don't look too excited about it."

I tried my best to look happy.

"It's just that the school year is only beginning, and I was looking forward to getting off to a good start. Going to Japan is a big deal. I don't even know anything about the place!"

I turned and ran up the stairs, shutting my door behind me. I flopped onto my bed. Ellsworth fell off as my head hit the pillow.

"Oh, I'm sorry, Ellsworth," I said, picking the bear up off the floor. "Dad just told me we're going

14

to Japan, and I really don't want to."

I looked into his eyes. I could see a tiny picture of my face reflected in each one. I stared back at myself. *Why am I so upset?* I thought. Usually, I like traveling, but for some reason, I was worried about this trip.

There was a knock on the door.

"Hope? May I come in?" came Dad's voice.

"C'mon in," I said.

He sat down on the side of my bed. "Well, did Ellsworth have any words of wisdom for you?"

"Not really," I said. "I guess I'm just scared about taking a trip to someplace so far away."

"You've never been scared before," Dad said. "Why now?"

"I don't know. I'm scared about the plane crashing, or maybe a fire burning down our house while we're gone . . . or . . ."

Then I realized what was bothering me.

"Wasn't Japan where they had that awful earthquake a few years ago?"

"Yes, but you were pretty young when that happened. I'm surprised you remember," Dad said.

"I just remember Mom being worried about her friend Vicki. Wasn't she in Japan then?"

"She still is," Dad answered. "In fact, that's who you'll be staying with while I go to Tokyo to work with a business there. Your mother is really looking forward to seeing Vicki. She hasn't seen her since

15

they were roommates in college."

"What's she doing over there?" I asked.

"Vicki's an assistant English teacher at the high school in Nagoya. She helps the Japanese kids learn English," he explained.

"So she was OK during the earthquake?" I was still thinking about how scary an earthquake would be.

"She was fine. In fact, it happened in another city, so it didn't really affect her."

Dad took my hand and held it for a minute. He looked like he was thinking. "You know, Hope. There is danger everywhere. We could have an earthquake right here, in fact . . . or a tornado or some other terrible thing. We can't escape danger. But we can't let that get in the way of enjoying what there is to enjoy. We have to believe that God will take care of us. He doesn't promise to always keep us out of danger, but He does promise to help us through it."

I knew Dad was right. I just had a hard time not worrying sometimes. "Don't you ever worry?" I asked.

"At times I do, but I know it's not the right thing to do. Think of it this way, Hope. You know those bullet-proof vests that some policemen wear?"

"You mean the ones that protect their bodies if someone shoots at them?" I asked.

"Yes. Wearing the vest doesn't stop the accident,

but it can save a policeman's life. In the same way, God puts himself between you and the hurt. He may not always take away the danger or the pain, but He places himself between you and it so that it won't be so bad. You don't need to worry because God is always with us. Does that help?"

"Yes, it helps a lot."

"So . . . do you think you're ready to go to Japan?"

Chapter Two

Annie, you're dripping your ice cream all over me," I said, wiping the drips off my leg.

"I can't help it. It's hard to eat and look at the same time," she complained.

"Look to the right. We're passing Mount Fuji," Dad said. I stared out the window of the train. I couldn't believe we had already made it safely to Japan. Beside us was a huge, snow-covered mountain. It was hard to imagine that at one time, that same mountain had spit hot lava.

"Look fast, girls, or you'll miss it!" Mom joked.

"How fast are we going anyway?" I asked.

"The train goes up to 150 miles an hour," Dad said. "That's why they call this the bullet train."

"I can't get over how quiet and clean it is," Mom added.

"Clean it *was*, you mean," I said. "At least until Annie bought her ice cream. It's all over the place!"

I watched the attendant as he neared our seats.

Leaning over to Annie, I said, "I hope he's not going to yell at us for making such a mess."

He had on a navy blue hat and was wearing white gloves. He was pushing a cart down the aisle. It was filled with lunch food, drinks, and ice cream.

"Can I have another ice cream?" Annie asked Mom.

I couldn't believe my ears!

"I think one is more than enough, Annie," Mom said.

After we passed Mount Fuji, Dad fell asleep. Mom was reading a magazine. Annie and I decided to get up and stretch a little. As I stood up and started to walk, I noticed it felt like the train wasn't even moving. It was the smoothest ride I had ever been on.

I whispered into Annie's ear, "You know, we're the only ones with light hair on this whole train."

Every other person's hair was black. I guess Annie was so busy looking at everyone's hair that she didn't notice the attendant coming back carrying a glass of something.

"Watch out, Annie!" I shouted. It was too late. She ran right into the attendant.

Now her ice-cream-stained dress was also covered with orange juice! The attendant hurried back

20

to his cart and returned with a warm, damp cloth. He used it to soak up most of the juice, saying, "I very sorry. I think you going to stop, but you keep going."

When the attendant finished cleaning up, he bowed low to Annie and said he was sorry again. She bowed back and said it was OK. He then bowed again. Annie bowed, too.

I leaned over to her. "Stop bowing!" I said.

She turned and ran back to Mom and Dad. I smiled at the attendant and bowed slightly. Then *I* ran, too!

We reached our seats, out of breath. Dad was awake now.

"Well, girls, did you get yourselves all cleaned up?"

"Kind of," I said, looking over at Annie's very wet dress.

"You're soaked! You actually look worse than when you left," Mom said. "What did you do? Take a bath?"

"Not exactly," Annie said.

"Let's just say she ran into a little trouble," I added.

The last part of our trip took us to a little town west of Nagoya called Tsu (Sue) City. This was

where we would meet up with Mom's friend Vicki Thomas. Dad was going to stay the night with us, then go to Tokyo for a few days on business. Mom said that Miss Thomas had some neat things planned for us to do while we were in town.

"There she is!" Mom said, pressing her hand against the train window. "She's hardly changed at all."

I looked over to see a short, dark-haired woman wearing a pink dress and carrying a bunch of yellow flowers.

"I'd recognize her anywhere. She always did look great in pink!" Mom said. By then, she was hardly able to sit still. She had grabbed her purse and was heading out the door.

"You get the rest of the things," she said. "I'll meet you out there."

Suddenly, her light brown hair blended into the crowd. I lost sight of her.

Dad laughed. "Your mom isn't anxious or anything, is she? She's acting like she's nineteen again!"

I looked out of the window and saw Mom rushing toward her friend. They were hugging each other so tightly, I thought Miss Thomas would drop the flowers she was holding.

A few minutes later, we were standing on the platform with all our things. Mom was introducing us.

"This is Hope, the oldest. And this is Annie,"

she said. "Of course, you remember Reid. He was always teasing you."

Dad reached over and hugged Miss Thomas. "It's good to see you, Vicki. It's been a long time."

"Who would've guessed we would meet here in Japan!" Miss Thomas said.

Miss Thomas suggested we take a taxi home. "I usually walk or ride my bike, but with all your luggage, it would be a real trick."

"You mean you don't have a car?" I asked.

"I don't need a car here," she said. "I can get everywhere I need to with my own legs and the trains."

"But what do you do on days when it's raining?" Annie asked.

"I take an umbrella!" Vicki answered with a wink.

When we got out of the taxi, Miss Thomas said we were going to the eighth floor of the apartment building.

"It's not a very big apartment," she said. "But I really like the view. You can see the Pacific Ocean and Tsu City."

Annie laughed. "When you say Tsu City, it sounds like you're talking about my friend Sue in Chicago."

"We're a long way from Chicago," she said. "But it does sound almost the same!"

I looked out of the window toward the water. It

looked so calm—as smooth as the ride on the train.

Miss Thomas came up behind me. "It's beautiful, isn't it? There is something very peaceful about Japan."

I looked down at the buildings. For just a second, I thought about how scary it would be if the earth started to shake and everything started to crumble. I tried to make the thought go away, but it crept in anyway. For a second, I was really frightened.

Miss Thomas was still standing next to me. "Hope?" she said. "If you'd like to wash up, I'll put on some tea. Then we'll sit down and talk about our plans for the next few days."

I had a feeling the next few days wouldn't go as planned!

Chapter Three

A re you sure it will be all right to have Hope and Annie go to school with Midori?" Mom asked. "She doesn't even know us."

"It'll be fine, Gail," Miss Thomas said. "I know her sister, Yoko, very well—she's one of my best students in the high school—and I have already talked to Midori's teachers. Both Hope and Annie may stay with Midori in her third-grade class. There are several teachers at the school who speak perfect English. They can help the girls if they have any trouble."

"What do you think, girls?"

Annie was more excited than I was. I wasn't sure I wanted to spend the whole day away from Mom.

Mom could tell I was worried.

"If you don't want to, Hope, you don't have to.

I just thought it might be fun for you to see what it's like to go to school in Japan," Mom said.

"Oh, c'mon, Hope," Miss Thomas added. "It'll be an adventure. You might even learn a little Japanese!"

I was sure that wasn't possible. I had never heard a language where the words sounded so sharp and short. Everyone talked so fast in Japan!

I finally said I'd go, but only if I could count it as a school day for me.

"Of course," Dad said. "Just because you aren't hearing the lessons in English doesn't mean you're not learning something!"

With that settled, Miss Thomas suggested taking us out to a Japanese restaurant around the corner. "We're going to meet Yoko's family there, so you can get to know them."

A short walk around the corner, and we were at the restaurant. The Nakagawas weren't there yet. We took our seats.

Right away, a waitress came and put warm wash cloths in front of us. I waited to see what Miss Thomas would do with hers.

She picked up her cloth and began to wipe her hands. I did the same thing.

"This is for cleaning your hands before you eat," she explained. "It's a kindness the restaurant does."

"It feels good," Annie said, putting the cloth to her cheek.

"It's not for washing your face, sweetie," Dad said. "But we'll pretend you didn't know." He winked.

Annie looked a little hurt. "I just like the way it feels, that's all."

While Dad ordered for us, Annie and I opened our chopsticks and tried to figure out how we were going to pick up anything with them.

Just then the Nakagawas came in. Yoko had long, straight black hair. She smiled sweetly as she introduced her sister, Midori, and her mother and father.

Midori was small for an eight-year-old, I thought. Her dark hair was cut short with thick bangs across her forehead.

Mr. Nakagawa was small, too. He had to look way up to talk to Dad. Mrs. Nakagawa was quiet and kept her hands clasped in front of her. Of course, they all bowed politely. I bowed, too. I was still puzzled about when to stop bowing.

Once we all sat down, Miss Thomas asked Yoko if she would tell Annie and me how to use chopsticks.

"Of course. Hold the first chopstick like you're holding a pencil. Then slide the other one underneath it," Yoko said in perfect English.

We both tried. At least we got a good hold before we dropped them again.

"Maybe you should wait until your food comes." Mom laughed.

"I ordered some Japanese food for you to try. If you don't like it, you don't have to eat it. I think you'll find something you enjoy, though," Dad said.

The waitress came with bowls of soup.

"Nice, warm soup sounds good right about now," Mom said. "I'm pretty tired of airplane food."

Miss Thomas smiled. "Well, you might think differently in a minute."

We all dipped our spoons in and took a gulp of the warm soup.

"Yuk!" Annie said in a rather loud voice. "What's in this stuff?"

Everyone laughed except for Mr. Nakagawa. He shot a stern glance at Annie.

"That's *miso* soup," Miss Thomas laughed. "A lot of people eat it for breakfast. It's made of soybean paste and hot water."

"And seaweed," Yoko added.

"Seaweed! No thanks," I said, pushing my bowl away from me.

"Sorry about that, girls," Dad said. "Maybe you'll like what comes next better."

The waitress brought small teapots for each of us and placed a little cup next to each pot.

"Where are the cup handles?" Annie asked.

"There are no handles," Miss Thomas explained.

She picked hers up with both hands, holding it close to the rim. "If you don't fill your cup too full, you can enjoy your tea without burning your fingers. Try it."

I liked the tea. Better yet, I didn't spill any when I poured.

Soon the waitress returned with many plates of food. The plate in front of Dad looked the most interesting.

"I don't know why you like raw fish, Reid," Mom said, trying to hold on to her chicken with chopsticks.

"It's easier to eat *sushi* (soo-she) with chopsticks than what you ordered!" he bragged.

Mom started laughing as she tried to catch the egg and rice between her chopsticks.

I kind of liked my food. I picked up one of the shrimp in my chopsticks and started to hand it over to Annie. She held out her chopsticks to take it from me. Suddenly, the restaurant got quiet.

Mr. Nakagawa waved his hands. "No, no!"

People were staring at us. Annie and I dropped our chopsticks. Annie's face was redder than her hair.

"What did we do wrong?" I asked.

"It's hard to explain," Miss Thomas said. "Touching chopsticks together like that happens only during a Buddhist funeral. It's very important to the Japanese to never touch pairs of chopsticks together except in that ceremony."

"I'm sorry," I said. I wasn't even sure what a Buddhist was.

I looked at Mr. Nakagawa. He looked very stern and upset. "I'm sorry, sir," I said.

"You didn't know," Miss Thomas said.

I looked around the room at all the faces of the people. This was a very different country. There was *a lot* I didn't know.

Chapter Four

Early the next day, we got on the train again. We were going with Dad back to Nagoya, where Miss Thomas taught high school. Dad would go on to Tokyo and meet us back in Tsu City in a couple of days.

"I hope you girls enjoy your time with Mom and Miss Thomas," he said as we neared the station in Nagoya. "I will see you soon."

When we said good-bye, I hugged Dad extra long.

"It will be OK, Hope. Keep remembering what we talked about at home. I've got to go."

Dad rushed off to catch another train to Tokyo. Home seemed very far away right then.

"First, we'll stop by the high school," Miss Thomas said. "I've got a substitute teacher for my class, but I want to show you around my school. We might even see Yoko."

"How long have you known Yoko?" I asked.

"Well," Miss Thomas began, "she came to Nagoya High from Tsu City after finishing sixth grade. I'll never forget the first day I met her. She was going to be one of my English students. She had already taught herself English so well that she was better than many of the Japanese English teachers! She's also good at singing and sports. In fact, she's very good at everything she tries to do."

"Isn't Nagoya a long way to travel just to go to school?" Annie asked.

"It is," Miss Thomas said. "But school is very important to the Japanese. Getting a good education is almost more important than anything else. How you do in school decides where you go to college. Where you go to college decides what kind of job you will get. In fact, it decides your whole future. There's lots of pressure on children to make the best grades in school.

"You see those bicycles there by the station?" Miss Thomas asked. "Yoko rides her bike from home to the train station in Tsu City. She then rides the train to Nagoya and picks up another bike here at the station and rides it to school. She does that both ways."

"That must take hours!" I exclaimed.

"It's a sacrifice she is willing to make. She is in

tenth grade now. She is busy with school, home-work, and something called *juku* or 'cram school.' "

"What's that?" Annie asked.

"It's an evening class she takes to get ready for college entrance tests. I wouldn't be surprised if Midori is going to extra evening math classes, too."

"Sounds like Japanese students work awfully hard," Mom said.

"That's the truth." Miss Thomas nodded. "It's a lot different from the United States, where almost anyone can get into a college."

Just then a girl riding by on a bicycle stopped and called out to Miss Thomas. It was Yoko!

"Thomas *sensei*! Thomas sensei!"

Miss Thomas leaned over and explained that sensei (sen-say) means teacher.

"Hello, Yoko! We were just talking about you," Miss Thomas said in a cheery voice.

Yoko placed one foot down on the pavement to steady her bike and bowed her head. "I'm sorry about what happened at dinner last night. You must forgive my father," she said.

"It couldn't be helped, Yoko," Miss Thomas replied kindly.

Yoko changed the subject. "I heard you were not coming to school today, Thomas sensei. But here you are."

"I'm just stopping by to collect a few things before showing my friends around Nagoya. I will see

35

you tomorrow. Hope and Annie will be going to school with Midori tomorrow."

"Until then," Yoko said. She jumped back onto her seat and pedaled off. Many other bicyclists in blue-and-white uniforms were also pedaling to school.

Miss Thomas leaned over to me. "I see you watching that clump of bicyclists. In Japan, people like to work and play in groups. They do almost everything in groups. Yoko, though, has a mind of her own. She's a strong young lady."

―――――――

When we got to Nagoya High School, we headed straight for the teachers' lounge. The room was filled with desks. To me, it looked like a classroom.

"This is strange," Mom said. "I never saw anything like this back in the States when I was teaching."

"That's because we do it differently here," Miss Thomas said. "Every morning we teachers sit at our own desks and talk to one another about the students we have and our plans for the day. Everything we do is planned around the students."

Miss Thomas took us around and introduced us to many of the teachers. They were excited to practice their English on us.

"If Japanese teachers came to visit a school in the

States, very few teachers would be practicing their Japanese with them," Mom said. "You know, Vicki, it's sad that most Americans can speak only one language."

Annie spoke up. "I think it's neat that Miss Thomas can speak Japanese. When I get home, I'm going to start learning."

"Why wait until then?" Miss Thomas said. "Here's your first Japanese word. *Konnichiwa* (Konnee-chee-wa). It means hello or good morning."

For the rest of the day, Annie said hello to everyone she met. When we walked in the shopping center, she bowed and said hello to the white-gloved attendants. When we climbed in the elevator, she bowed to the elevator attendant. And when we ate lunch, she said hello to the waiters and the other customers. By the time the day was over, I was tired of hearing the word hello.

"Maybe you could teach her another word tomorrow?" I suggested to Miss Thomas.

I hated to think about tomorrow. *School with Midori*. Deep down, I was worried about tomorrow.

Chapter Five

When we got back to the apartment that night, I could hardly sleep. I was really nervous about being in Japanese school all day and away from Mom. I had never even spent a day in an American school, let alone a Japanese one. What if something happened while we were there? What if I got sick? What if I got lost?

I lay awake and hugged Ellsworth.

"I wish I could bring you with me tomorrow, but they'd probably make fun of me if I did. I'm trying really hard not to be scared, but I'm not sure I can do this."

I looked over at Annie sleeping peacefully on the futon next to me.

"I don't understand how she does it," I whispered to Ellsworth. "She never seems to be scared of anything. If only . . ."

<hr />

The next thing I heard was Mom's voice.

"Hope, you need to wake up. We have to be going soon."

It seemed awfully early. Mom helped me up from the bed and handed me some clothes.

"We are going to walk over to Midori's house so you can walk to school with her from there," she said.

I wriggled into my clothes and picked up Ellsworth. "Maybe if I stuff you way under my other things in the backpack, no one will notice," I told him.

I took out all of my books and squeezed Ellsworth into the bottom of the backpack. "Sorry about the tight squeeze, but I'm sure you can bear it," I said, trying to sound happy.

Mom called from the other room. "C'mon, Hope, Annie. We need to be on our way."

I grabbed my books and placed them gently on the top of my bear before heading out the door.

<hr />

The Nakagawas' house was right in the middle

of Tsu City. In fact, you had to walk through a store to get into the house.

"Don't forget to take your shoes off every time you go into the house," Miss Thomas reminded us. "There are slippers for you to put on." I looked at Annie, remembering the day at the bus stop when she wore her slippers outside.

When we got there, Midori was waiting for us. Yoko had already left for school hours ago.

We all three bowed. Then Miss Thomas gave us a piece of paper to give to Midori's teacher.

"Are you sure they'll be all right?" Mom asked her. "I think we should walk them to the school just to be sure."

"Relax, Gail," she said. "Japan has some of the safest streets in the world. They will be walking with lots of other children who know just where to go. They won't stray. They'll stay right with the group."

I remembered what Miss Thomas had mentioned to us about groups yesterday.

We said good-bye to Mom and Miss Thomas and promised we'd be back right after school at three o'clock.

Annie and I held hands and started off down the road past all the stores and shops. I was surprised that the school looked old and not at all like the new schools at home.

Midori led us to her classroom, where we sat down and waited for the teacher.

"I feel like everyone is staring at us," I said to Annie.

"Just say hello in Japanese and everything will be fine," Annie said.

I looked at the nearly forty students and braced myself for Annie's hellos.

Just then the teacher came in. I handed her the card Miss Thomas had given to me.

"Welcome to our school. My name is Araki sensei," she said after reading the card. "I glad you could be here to visit. If you like to take seat, we will start day now."

I noticed that Miss Araki didn't speak English as well as Yoko. I was beginning to see what Miss Thomas meant about Yoko being special.

Most of the morning was spent working on two things: handwriting and math. Handwriting looked more like art class to me. They used brushes instead of pencils, and the letters were made up of curves, dots, and lines.

Midori grew very serious when she worked on math. Each child used a wooden frame with beads on it. The clicking of the beads sounded like music.

"Maybe we should work on our own math problems," I said to Annie.

Annie took out some work sheets Mom had given us.

"These might as well be in Japanese," Annie whispered. "I'm never going to be good at math."

42

In between math and writing, we took a short break to move around and get some exercise. As soon as the teacher called the class to order, the students took their seats.

The afternoon went so fast I could hardly believe it was time to go. As Midori, Annie, and I walked with the others in the group, I wanted to race ahead. I couldn't wait to talk to Mom.

We rushed through the shop and into the house.

I stopped. "Shoes! Shoes!" I yelled to Annie. She ran ahead.

In the time it took me to take off my shoes and put down my backpack, Annie was already telling Mom everything.

"So what was your favorite part, Hope?" Mom asked me when I walked in with Midori.

"Lunch and clean-up time, they—"

"During lunch, the teacher sat at the desk, and the students served each other!" Annie interrupted.

"Annie! She asked me." I looked at Mom. "Some of the children put on aprons and hats and handed out milk, chopsticks, and damp towels like we had at the restaurant."

"This time, we knew what to do with the chopsticks," Annie said.

"You mean, what *not* to do," Miss Thomas said with a wink.

"You were right about school, Miss Thomas," I began. "I couldn't believe how well everyone worked together. It made—"

"The most fun was getting to clean the bathrooms!" Annie broke in again.

I wasn't about to let Annie tell all the good stories.

"It was great," I said. "Annie and I cleaned the floors. Midori and Annie sat on a big towel, and I pulled them on it to dry the floor. It was so much fun!" I said.

"I hardly know what to think," Mom said. "It's been a long time since I heard anyone get excited over cleaning a bathroom!"

"It's all part of working together as a team," Miss Thomas explained. "Besides, we don't have any trouble here with children writing on walls or throwing things on the floors. They're the ones who have to clean it up!"

"I admit you have a point," Mom said.

She hugged us both again. "Well, I'm glad everything went well."

"Mrs. Nakagawa wondered if you'd like to stay and visit with Midori for a while," Miss Thomas said. "We're waiting until Yoko gets home from school."

We both wanted to see Yoko.

"Midori can show you around the house and the shop while we wait," Miss Thomas said. "Just don't touch anything."

For the first time since we had arrived at Midori's

house, I started looking around. I knew that we had walked through a store of some kind before coming into the house, but I hadn't paid much attention to it.

Annie and I followed Midori back out to the front of the house where the shop was.

"What are these things anyway?" Annie asked me.

"I'm not sure. They sure do look fancy, though."

Midori walked over to one of the big black pieces of furniture and pointed to the gold painting on the side.

Annie reached up and touched the paint.

"No!" Midori yelled.

Quickly, Annie pulled her hand back.

I looked behind me and saw Mr. Nakagawa coming toward us. It was all I could do to keep my legs from shaking.

He stood still and looked straight at Midori. His eyebrows formed a sharp angle on his forehead. She stepped back and said something to her father, bending low. Mr. Nakagawa scowled. Midori motioned to us to leave. Annie and I practically ran out of the room.

I was glad Mr. Nakagawa stayed in the store. The kitchen felt safer without him.

"Midori and I are going upstairs to her room. You want to come?" Annie asked.

"No thanks," I said. "I'll stay down here with Miss Thomas and Mom."

As soon as they left, I asked Miss Thomas what the store sold.

"It's a place to display Buddhist and Shinto altars," she said.

There was that word *Buddhist* again. What was she talking about?

"What are those? What do you do with them?"

"Well," she explained, "many Japanese families have a family altar at home. At night, they kneel down together and say evening prayers to Buddha. Usually, there are candlesticks and incense on the altars and a picture of Buddha. You can put what you want on the altar."

"So is Buddha like God to them?" I asked.

"Sort of," she said. "It's hard to explain. Most Japanese worship more than one god. Many worship the goddess of the sun—Shinto—and Buddha."

"They often mix religions and follow what they've been taught by their parents," Mom said.

"What if they choose not to believe in Buddha or Shinto?" I asked.

"They don't have that choice. Not following the tradition of your parents is to dishonor your family," Miss Thomas said. "That's something the Japanese just don't do."

46

At that moment, Yoko walked into the kitchen. Her father was standing right next to her. "Father would like to speak to you, Miss Thomas," she said.

I decided it was time for me to leave.

Chapter Six

I walked through the kitchen and into what looked like the dining room. There was a low table, some pillows on the floor, and a TV. The floor felt like twisted straw. Where was Midori's room?

All the inside walls of the house were made of a thick paper—so thick, you couldn't see through it. The walls slid back and forth like doors.

This house was sure confusing. I was feeling very lost. I could hear a TV somewhere. *Annie and Midori must be watching TV*, I thought. I walked up a stairway and into a room with two beds and another TV. No one. I walked through two more rooms with TVs before I finally found Midori and Annie watching TV in Midori's room.

"I thought I'd never find you," I said to Annie.

"This house is sure strange. I've never seen so many TVs in one place!"

"Shhh," Annie said. "I want to hear what's going on."

"As if you can understand it!" I laughed.

"Oh, oh!" Annie exclaimed, bouncing up and down. "He just said 'Hello'! I heard him. Hope, do you know what this means? I can speak Japanese! I can speak two languages!"

I rolled my eyes and sat down on the floor. "I suppose it's a start, Annie."

———————

A little while later, Mom called us downstairs.

"Yoko and Vicki said that if you'd like to stay overnight here, you could sleep over. We could come after breakfast and pick you up. What do you think?"

I already knew my answer. No way!

But Annie was jumping up and down. "That would be so much fun. Oh, please! Can we?"

Mom looked at me. "Well, it depends on Hope. I would enjoy going out alone with Vicki this evening, but I don't want you to feel like you have to stay here. I'd be glad to drop off some of your clothes before we head out for dinner. I'd even bring Ellsworth for you, Hope."

"That's not necessary, Mom," I said, not wanting to tell her that I had him all along.

I could tell I was outnumbered. Both Mom and Annie wanted it to work out. If I said no now, I would be wrecking things for everyone.

"I guess it's all right," I said.

"Great! I'll drop off your clothes and pajamas in about an hour. I'm sure you'll have a great time," Mom said. "Remember, if you have any trouble, just talk to Yoko."

As soon as Mom and Miss Thomas left, I had the same scared feeling I had the day Dad told me that we were going to Japan.

Yoko must have seen I was upset because she showed me into the room with the table. "Would you like a tangerine? They are very good," she said, handing me one.

"Thank you," I said, trying to be polite.

"It's too bad you couldn't have been here for one of our festivals. We have some wonderful celebrations here in Tsu City. My favorite one is the Tsu Festival in October. People everywhere sell sweets, popcorn, baked apples, and soy sauce on grilled corn. There's a parade and music, and children take turns carrying a shrine as they walk through the town."

"You mean a shrine like in the front of your shop?" I asked.

"Kind of like that. The shrines rest on sticks so children can carry them above their heads."

"What does it mean?"

Yoko thought for a minute. "I don't know if it means anything. It's just fun."

I thought her Japanese religion was as confusing as her Japanese house.

It was as if she read my mind. "Do you want me to show you around the house? I don't want you to get lost."

I followed her outside the house to the bathroom.

"This is an old house," Yoko explained. "When I was little, I did not like going downstairs and then outside in the middle of the night to go to the bathroom. My grandparents used to live down here." She pointed to another room.

"They are both dead now, but when I was little, I would visit them all the time. If I had to go downstairs in the night, I would just stay down here with them afterward. Sometimes I think my house can be kind of scary."

"Do you ever have earthquakes?" I asked. I figured we might as well talk about all the scary stuff at once.

"Oh yes. All the time," she said matter-of-factly. "But you get used to it."

"I don't think I'd ever get used to them," I said. "Doesn't the ground split open and swallow people?"

"It hasn't swallowed me yet," Yoko said, laughing. "You just have to be careful about things falling on top of you during an earthquake. That's why everything in our house is so lightweight."

She stood next to one of the screen doors and pushed it back and forth. "If one of these doors falls on top of you, it doesn't hurt very much!"

I put my hand on one of the panels and pushed a little. To my surprise, I punched a hole in it!

"Oh no!" I said. "What happened?"

Yoko had her hand up to her mouth in surprise. "Oh dear."

"How did this happen?" I said. "I barely pushed on it."

Yoko took a long look. "This one has been repaired several times already. Midori put a hole through it with a ball once. It's not your fault."

I was so embarrassed. Just then would have been a great time for an earthquake to come and swallow me up!

"Don't worry, Hope," Yoko said. "I'll take care of it."

At that moment, Annie and Midori came into the room. Midori gasped when she saw the hole.

I felt like I wanted to cry.

Annie stood next to me. "What happened, Hope?"

"I accidentally put a hole in the screen. I think I'm going to be in trouble."

We heard Mrs. Nakagawa coming. Yoko hurried to where she was, then motioned for us to follow. I think she was afraid her mother might see the door.

We all walked to the table and sat down on the floor quietly. Yoko explained that we needed to sit with our knees bent and our legs tucked under us.

"Do not sit sideways or let your legs come out from beneath you. Only men are allowed to sit like that," she said. "Father gets very angry if we do."

As Yoko spoke, Mr. Nakagawa came in and sat down. He didn't smile. He simply bowed and sat, too.

How am I going to tell him what happened? I can't even speak his language! I thought.

Mrs. Nakagawa served us tea and a chicken and rice dish. She smiled a lot and seemed very nice.

"Mother asks if you are enjoying your stay," Yoko said.

"Yes, very much," I said, trying to hide how I really felt. "Tell her the food is very good."

Yoko said something in Japanese, and her mother smiled back and bowed her head. Yoko then turned to her father and spoke. Midori looked frightened.

As Yoko spoke, Mr. Nakagawa stopped chewing. He looked very mad. *She must be telling him about the door*, I thought. I couldn't understand why he was not mad at me. Instead, he was speaking very loudly to Yoko.

Yoko bowed her head and was silent. No one said anything more. Mr. Nakagawa got up from the table and left, and Mrs. Nakagawa started clearing the table. At last, Yoko spoke.

"I'm sorry about that. I thought I should tell Father about the door before he found it. I didn't want him to think we were hiding it," she said.

"But I did it. Why was he yelling at you?" I asked.

"He assumed *I* did it," Yoko said.

"But that's terrible," I said. "You shouldn't take the blame for something you didn't do."

"That's OK, Hope," Yoko said. "Father doesn't like anything I do anyway. He thinks I'm a bad person . . . 'the rebel,' he calls me. One more thing isn't going to make much difference."

"I'm sorry," I said.

"It's OK. Listen. I have to go out tonight. I'll be back kind of late, but I think you'll be OK if you and Annie just stick with Midori and stay up in her room. I probably won't see you in the morning because I have to leave for school really early, before you even get up."

"You have school on Saturday?" Annie asked.

"Yes, until noon. But maybe we'll see one another again before you leave," she said.

Yoko got up from the table. "Don't worry, Hope. Everything will be OK."

I wasn't so sure.

Chapter Seven

Midori pointed to the mattress on the floor. I knew she meant I would be sleeping there. Annie was going to sleep next to me.

The TV was on, and we watched a show where women were fighting with long sticks. It kind of looked like sword fighting. Of course, I couldn't understand anything they were saying.

Midori took out a piece of string and wrapped it around both hands.

"She wants to play cat's cradle," Annie said.

I placed my fingers inside the web of string and smiled at Midori. "Now this I understand."

We spent a long time passing the string back and forth from each other's hands. I made a cup and saucer.

Midori turned it upside down.

"Now it looks just like a Japanese house!" Annie laughed.

Then Midori took the string and showed us beautiful dragonflies and butterflies.

"She's very quick!" I said to Annie.

I was glad we had something in common.

While we were playing, Mr. and Mrs. Nakagawa came up and motioned to us to follow them. We all filed out of the room and walked to an altar not far from their bedroom. Mr. Nakagawa lit a candle.

"It smells like spices in here," Annie whispered to me.

Then Mr. and Mrs. Nakagawa knelt down and bowed low to the floor. Midori sat behind them and did the same.

Annie and I looked at each other. We didn't know what to do. We stood and waited.

After the prayer, they stood up. Mr. and Mrs. Nakagawa bowed to us. I wondered if Mr. Nakagawa would have bowed to me if he knew I was the one who put a hole in the screen.

"I'm tired," Annie said.

"Me too. Midori has an early morning, so we should probably get to bed," I agreed.

We all got our pajamas on and got under our covers. I pulled Ellsworth out of my backpack and put him next to me. I noticed Midori had a special stuffed animal she took to bed with her, too. I guess we weren't that different.

When the lights were out, it was very quiet.

Where's Yoko? She wasn't there for the family altar time. I thought about how she said her dad called her a rebel. Why?

I looked over at Midori. She was already asleep.

"Annie?"

"Yes, Hope."

"Do you think Yoko seems like a bad person?"

"No. Why would you say that?"

"Well, she said her dad calls her a rebel."

"What's a rebel?" Annie asked.

"It's someone who doesn't do what she's told to do."

"I wonder where she goes at night," Annie said.

"I don't know."

We both lay there in the strange house. I didn't think I'd ever get to sleep.

"Annie?"

There was no answer. She was asleep, too!

Now I felt really alone. Hours must have passed. I heard the Nakagawas come upstairs. The television was on for a while, then I saw their lights go out. I knew Yoko was still not home. Her bedroom was right next to Midori's.

I held on to Ellsworth. Yoko was right. This was a scary place sometimes.

Suddenly, I heard something I didn't expect to hear. Crying! I sat up. Annie and Midori were both asleep. It sounded like it was coming from the room next door. *Yoko?* I hadn't heard her come in.

I got up quietly and walked over to the screen door. Carefully, I pushed it back. There was Yoko. She was sitting against a bookshelf, her knees up and her head down. She looked up when I came in. She started to wipe her eyes and tried to smile.

"What are you doing up so late, Hope?"

"I couldn't sleep. I thought I heard someone crying," I said.

I came close to her and noticed she smelled like smoke.

"I'm sorry if I woke you," she said. "I just got in from work."

"Work?" I said.

"Yes, I work at the coffee shop down the street. I help serve coffee and desserts."

I thought about her being a rebel. Was she telling the truth or making something up?

"So how did everything go tonight? Did you have fun with Midori?"

I told her about playing cat's cradle and about the family altar.

"Yes. I don't like to go to family altar."

"Is that why your father calls you a rebel?" I asked.

"That's a big part of it," Yoko said. "Hope, it's getting late. Maybe we can talk about this later. I need to go to bed so I can get up for school in the morning."

I said good-night and went back to my mat. Morning couldn't come soon enough for me!

Chapter Eight

I woke the next morning to the sound of chopping in the kitchen. I put on some clothes and raced downstairs, past the room where Mr. Nakagawa painted altars. The strong smell of paint mixed with the smell of eggs cooking.

Annie was already downstairs in the kitchen.

"Hi, Hope," she said. She looked rested.

How does she do that? I thought.

"Hi, Annie. Are Yoko and Midori already gone?"

"Yes, they left a while ago. Mrs. Nakagawa already fixed them breakfast. She's making more for us. I tasted Midori's—sugar and eggs rolled up like a jelly roll."

"How did Yoko seem today?"

"Fine," Annie said. "Why?"

"Just wondered."

As we sat down to eat, Mom and Miss Thomas came in. I could hardly wait for them to slip off their shoes before I hugged Mom around the waist.

"My goodness, Hope. You'd think I'd been gone for months!"

I didn't tell her it had felt like months to me. I just held her more tightly.

"Everything go OK?" Miss Thomas asked.

"It was great!" Annie chimed in. "You should see what I learned to make!"

She ran out of the room to get some string.

Mom looked down at me and rubbed my arm. "How about you, Hope?"

"I'm OK, I guess. Just a little tired. I had a hard time falling asleep."

"I thought you might," Mom said. "I was a little worried about you, so I said a prayer for you."

Miss Thomas added, "I thought maybe we could all go for a walk around the city today. We should plan to get to bed early tonight because of church in the morning. I just heard about a Japanese Christian church here that I would like to visit tomorrow. I've always gone into Nagoya for church."

Before leaving, we sat down for breakfast. Mrs. Nakagawa sat down with us. She and Miss Thomas had a long conversation while Annie showed Mom the new things she had learned with her string.

I watched Mrs. Nakagawa's face as she talked. She looked tired. I had noticed how much she worked. I never saw her sitting down. She was always cooking, serving food, cleaning, or doing laundry.

Before we left, I ran upstairs to get my things. I was always running in this house because I was afraid I would see Mr. Nakagawa. As I ran past the screen I had torn, I stopped. It had already been fixed.

When I reached the kitchen, I walked slowly in.

"All ready to go?" Mom said.

"I think so," I said.

We all bowed to Mrs. Nakagawa, then put on our shoes. As we walked through the shop, we passed Mr. Nakagawa. I didn't even look at him. I just kept on walking.

———

Once we got out on the street, I asked Miss Thomas what she was saying to Mrs. Nakagawa.

"Oh, she's just a little worried about Yoko," she said. "She thinks Yoko is getting into some kind of trouble. She says she doesn't come in until late at night and is gone early on Sundays and doesn't come back all day."

"Is she bad at school?" I asked.

"Bad? Yoko? Just the opposite. She's the perfect student. She does everything well. She gets good grades. She has a great attitude. I wish all my students were like Yoko."

"Speaking of students, let's get some learning in here," Mom said. "Hope and Annie would like to know a little about some of the holidays and celebrations in Tsu City, Vicki. Why don't you tell them about it?"

"Well, there's so much to tell," Miss Thomas said. "There are many festivals in Japan. There's the Tsu Festival, where children hold up shrines called *mikoshis*."

"Oh, Yoko already told us about that one, Miss Thomas," I said. "That's in October, isn't it?"

"Well, I'm impressed," she said. "Tell me more."

"What I don't understand," I said, "is why they do all the things they do at the festival. Yoko couldn't really explain it."

"It's interesting that you should bring that up, Hope," Miss Thomas said. "I had a hard time understanding that myself when I first came over. A perfect example is Christmas and New Year's Day.

"At Christmas, all the stores are decked out with Santa Claus and Christmas trees. They even play Christmas carols in all the stores."

Annie interrupted. "Are they celebrating Jesus' birth?"

"No, they are just celebrating," Miss Thomas said. "They have simply adopted American traditions.

"The same goes for New Year's Day. The whole month of December is spent getting ready for it. There are parties to get ready for, work to finish, cards to write, the house to clean, and special foods to be cooked."

"That sounds like a lot of work," I said.

"Especially for Mrs. Nakagawa and other mothers. They have to cook everything ahead of time so nothing has to be done on New Year's Day. But the evening before, the children and adults stay up late into the night and wait to hear the temple bells ring in the new year."

As we turned the corner, we faced a large building.

"Well, would you look at that," Mom said. "Here's the temple right here!"

"I'm supposed to be a tour guide, right?" Miss Thomas laughed.

She showed us the huge bell outside the temple and explained that on New Year's Eve people stand outside with a huge log and strike the bell as the priest counts.

"Each strike of the bell stands for a different sin," Miss Thomas said. "Buddhists believe there are 108 different sins."

"Does hitting the bell forgive them for their sins?" Annie asked.

"No, it just stands for hope for a better year next year," Miss Thomas answered.

She explained that the next day, the whole family went to the Buddhist Temple and the Shinto shrine to worship both gods.

"That gets kind of confusing," I said.

"That's probably why Yoko won't go anymore," Miss Thomas said. "Her mother said that Yoko would not come with them last holiday. Mr. Nakagawa is not happy with her unwillingness to obey."

"Yoko told me her father calls her a rebel," I said.

"That's because she doesn't follow the crowd," Miss Thomas replied. "There is an old Japanese proverb. It says, 'The nail that sticks up will be hammered down.'"

"Is Yoko like the nail that sticks up?" Annie asked.

"I'm afraid so, Annie."

"So what's going to happen to her?" I asked.

"I don't know, Hope. We can only pray that God will help her know what is right."

I thought about Mr. Nakagawa and shivered.

Chapter Nine

The next morning, we were in a big rush to get to church. Dad had come back late Saturday night and was planning to be with us for church. We were all leaving Monday morning for Chicago.

I wasn't sure what to expect. What I was sure of was that going to church was something I did for a good reason. I went because Jesus was my friend, and I knew He cared about *everything* in my life.

I only wished Yoko and Midori could understand how I felt about Jesus.

We were going to walk to church. As we headed down the road, I felt funny about being American. I didn't see many others going the same way.

"Are we going to be the only ones there?" I asked Miss Thomas.

"I don't think so," she said. "This church is

pastored by a Japanese man and his family. It's not a big church, but I think at least thirty people go to it."

"Thirty isn't very many," Annie said.

"For a country that's nearly all Buddhist, that's a lot," Dad said.

"Well, here we are," Miss Thomas said. She pointed us to some seats near the back.

The building was small. In the front, a man was leading the singing, and a woman standing next to him was signing.

"They must have some deaf people here," Annie whispered to me.

I could hear some people making noises that didn't sound quite like singing. To my right, there was a group that signed the songs.

"That must be them over there," I said to Annie.

After we sat down, the pastor read from the Bible. It's fun to listen to different languages and how they sound. Sometimes Annie and I like to make up our own language and talk to each other in stores.

Once in a while, people turn around and look at us like we're really from another country. Right then, I turned to Annie.

"Annie, bij wan kily por too?"

She caught on right away. "Ingo lictor mya minge."

We tried not to start laughing.

70

I leaned down to get a tissue from my purse. For a minute, I thought I saw someone familiar. Then I realized I had.

I whispered something in Miss Thomas's ear, and she turned her head. Yoko!

Yoko seemed as surprised as we were. During the next praise song, she came and sat down next to us.

"What are you doing here?" she said.

"What are *you* doing here?" I asked.

"I come here every Sunday. Don't tell my parents, though. They would not want me to be a part of the family anymore."

Everything started making sense. I realized now that Yoko was not a bad person—she was a Christian!

I couldn't wait to talk.

————

As soon as the church service was over, Miss Thomas and Yoko hugged.

"I knew there was a good reason you didn't attend family altar, Yoko. Why didn't you tell me?"

"I wasn't sure how to. I am still not sure when to tell people and when not to," she said.

"I understand," Miss Thomas said. "It is very hard to be a Christian here in Japan."

"You must come home for lunch with us, and we will talk. Your parents are very worried about you."

"I know they are," Yoko said. "And I'm not sure how to obey them and God at the same time."

We all walked down the street with Yoko. I wanted to hold her hand, but Annie got next to her first. We were all so proud to be her friend. I was glad to know she wasn't a bad person.

Yoko began to tell us her story.

"When I was a little girl, I went to a church down the street for Bible school on Sundays. My parents let me go. They thought it was all right to go hear stories about Daniel and David and Goliath. It wouldn't hurt me, they'd say. By the time I was twelve or thirteen, I was sure that I loved Jesus and wanted to be part of God's family. I read my Bible and prayed. In the last few years, I knew I could not keep going to the Buddhist temple and the Shinto shrines. I do not believe in many gods. I believe in only one."

Miss Thomas put her hand on Yoko's shoulder. "That must be hard for you. I know you love your family."

"I do love my family, but I love Jesus more," she said. "I have decided to follow Jesus—no matter what the cost."

We had reached Miss Thomas's apartment.

As we climbed the stairs, Miss Thomas put her arm around Yoko. "This is not going to be easy for you, Yoko. We will pray that your family accepts your decision."

Yoko spent the rest of the afternoon with us. She showed Annie and me how to do *origami*.

"I will make each of you a paper crane," she said.

As she folded the paper over and over, she told us the story of Sadako, the Japanese girl who was very sick. Sadako believed that if she made a thousand paper cranes, she would get well.

"Sadako never finished making the cranes before she died, but afterward, hundreds of children finished them for her," Yoko explained. "Today, there is a monument to Sadako at Peace Park in Hiroshima.

"She never gave up hope," Yoko said. "I will never give up hope, either."

As she handed me the crane, she told me how much she liked my name.

"Hope is such a pretty name," she said. "My name, Yoko, means 'child of the sun.' I like my name, too."

That evening, we said good-bye to Yoko and told her how happy we were to meet her.

"If you ever get to Chicago, look us up," Dad said.

"We'd be glad to have you stay with us," Mom added.

She said she would, then walked down the steps.

Little did I know we'd see her sooner than we thought!

Chapter Ten

K*nock! Knock! Knock!* Someone was at the door. It was nearly two o'clock in the morning. For a minute, I couldn't remember where I was. Then I realized I was at Miss Thomas's apartment.

Mom, Dad, Annie, and I were sleeping on mats in the same room. Dad got up and went into the living room.

"Be careful, Reid!" Mom warned.

But Miss Thomas had already answered the door. There, standing in the doorway, was Yoko. She almost fell into Miss Thomas's arms.

"Yoko, what happened?" she asked.

"It's father," she gasped. "He has sent me away. He will not let me live in the house anymore."

"But why?"

"I told him I had become a Christian," Yoko

said, sobbing. "He will not have me anymore."

"What about your mother?"

"My mother was crying and trying to change his mind. He would not listen."

Yoko sat on the couch and put her face in her hands. "I only want to do what is right. Help me to know what is right."

I couldn't tell if she was talking to us or praying.

"Let's get you a place to sleep. Then we'll decide what to do," Miss Thomas said.

———————

The next morning, we had to leave early to catch our train back to Tokyo. Dad woke us up and told us not to wake Yoko on the way out.

The night before seemed like a dream now. Seeing Yoko in the living room was proof it had really happened.

"What's going to happen to her?" I asked.

"I'm sure God will take care of her, just like He takes care of us," Dad said.

We had started out the door of the apartment when I remembered something.

"Just a minute!" I said, running back in. I grabbed the little paper crane Yoko had made me and placed it next to her.

"This is for you, Yoko," I whispered. "From Hope."

A few months later, back in Chicago, we got a letter and package from Yoko.

Dear Mr. and Mrs. Brown, Hope, and Annie,

I am sorry I did not to get to say good-bye that morning you left. As you know, it was a hard night. I thought my life was over. My family no longer wanted me.

Since then, I have been working hard at school to finish before Christmas. I want to come to America to finish high school. I have been living with Miss Thomas with my parents' permission. My mother and sister come to visit me once a week.

My father wrote and asked me to tell him if I had been baptized as a Christian. I didn't want to tell him I had because I was afraid he would not let my mother and sister visit me anymore. I also didn't want to lie. I didn't answer. He asked me in a letter again. I didn't answer.

I prayed to know what to do. Miss Thomas prayed. My church family prayed. My father sent me a letter yesterday and said he didn't want to know anymore. He sent me money to go to America to be an exchange student. He said he wants me to come back when I am finished.

I am so happy. It still hurts to be away from my family, but I know God is taking care of me.

Love,
Yoko

P.S. Inside is something special for Hope and Annie.

"Well, girls, go ahead and open them," Dad said, handing us each a little envelope.

Inside were two silver pins in the shape of a crane—one for Annie and one for me. I smiled. The crane pin would always remind me of how God took care of Yoko—and me.

The End